MW00758119

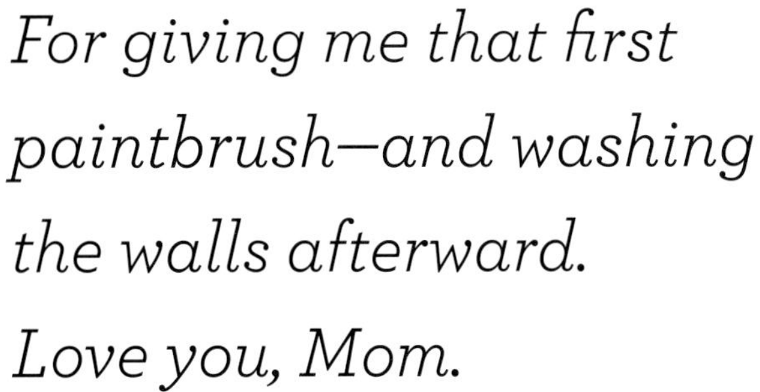

For giving me that first paintbrush—and washing the walls afterward. Love you, Mom.

Dial Books for Young Readers
Penguin Young Readers Group
An imprint of Penguin Random House LLC
375 Hudson Street
New York, NY 10014

Printed in China
ISBN 9780525427834

10 9 8 7 6 5 4 3 2 1

Design by Jasmin Rubero
Text set in Archer with Alboroto and Drawzing

The artwork was created with watercolors, charcoal, and colored pencils, with some digital assembly.

The Monster Next Door

David Soman

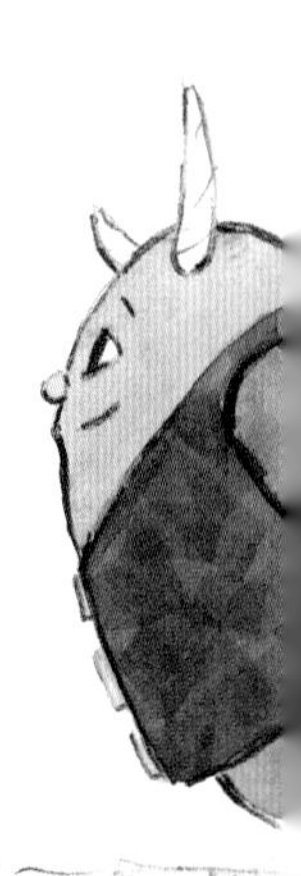

Dial Books for Young Readers

In a great big field,
a Boy had a tree house.

And one day, he had . . .

a neighbor.

said the Monster.

Who's there?

AREN'T YOU GLAD I DIDN'T SAY BANANA?

. . .

Okay. . .
Why did the chicken cross the road?

BURLAP!

Um . . .
No?

NOT BURLAP?

Uh . . . Do you want to play catch?

Ready?

GLOMP!

Whoa!

BLUURP!

Then the Monster
did a muscle pose.

So did the Boy.

The Boy did a silly dance.

The Monster did too.

When the Boy made a ridiculous face,

the Monster made an even ridiculouser one.

Then the Boy had an idea, and

the Monster caught on right away.

The Monster sent over a note.

The Boy sent one back.

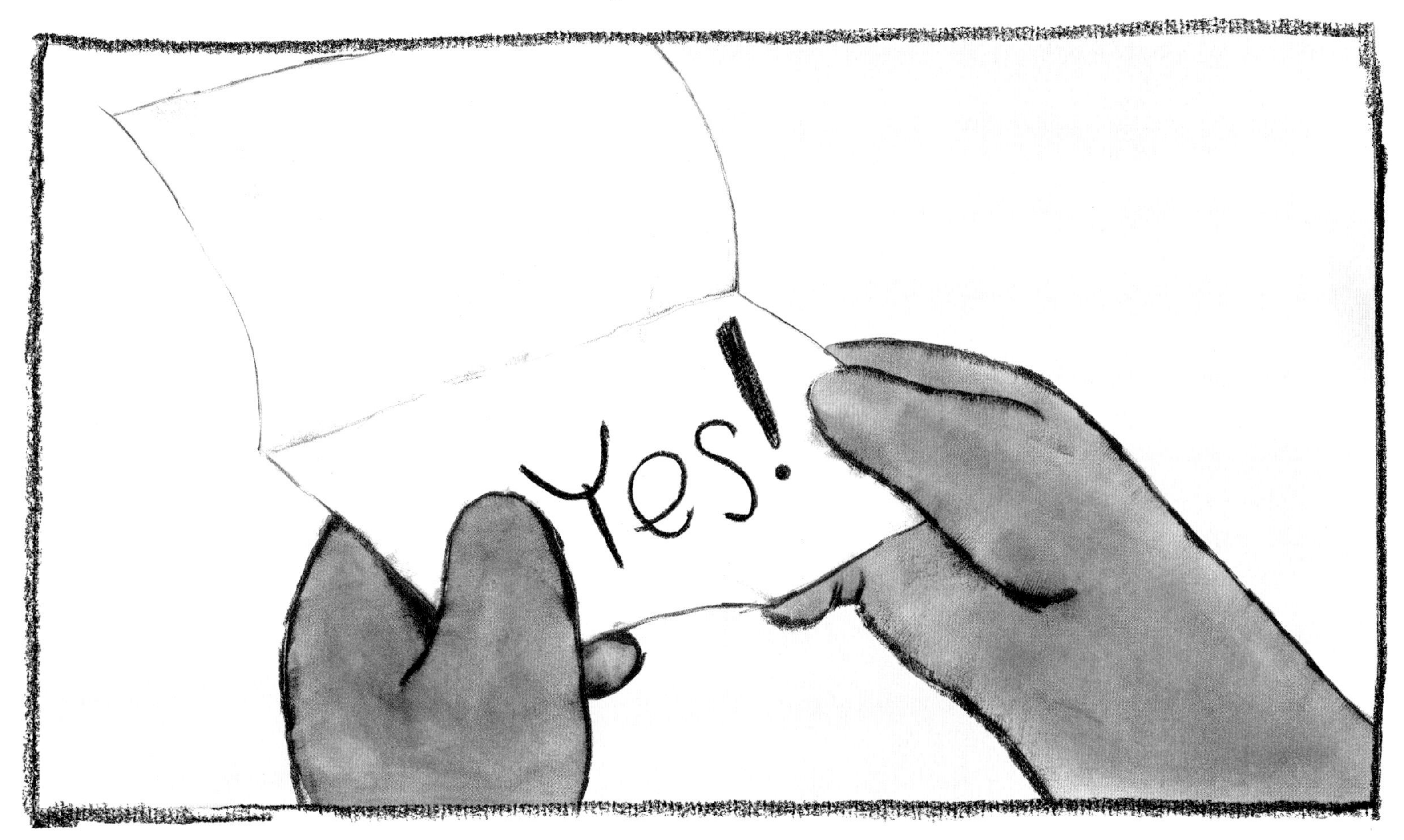

Everything was great.

This called
for music!

But . . .
HEY!

STOP IT! You're playing too loud!
yelled the Boy.

Still the Monster continued to play.

STOP PLAYING, YOU BIG PURPLE PIN-CUSHION!
WHAT?! YOU ARE A HOT DOG IN A HAT!
BONGO BRAIN!
FLIPPER FEET!
TURTLE NECK!
SNORKLE SNOUT!
WOMBAT!
BLOWFISH!
SLITHEY TOVE!
SNICKER SNACK!
RING DING!
DING DONG!

Without thinking, the Boy grabbed a water balloon.

SPLORT!

The Monster grabbed one too.

And so it went.

When the last balloon was thrown, the Boy took his scissors and cut the rope.

The bucket landed with an empty thud.

The Boy was so angry, he could think of only one thing to do.

He wrote to the Monster: NOT FRIENDS!

After all, the Monster had played too loud! He hadn't listened! He had thrown water balloons! He had even made the Boy cut the rope!
The Boy saw it clearly—

the Monster
was *mean.*

So the Boy marched over with his note.

Hello?
But there was no answer. He scowled. Now the Monster was even making him climb up!

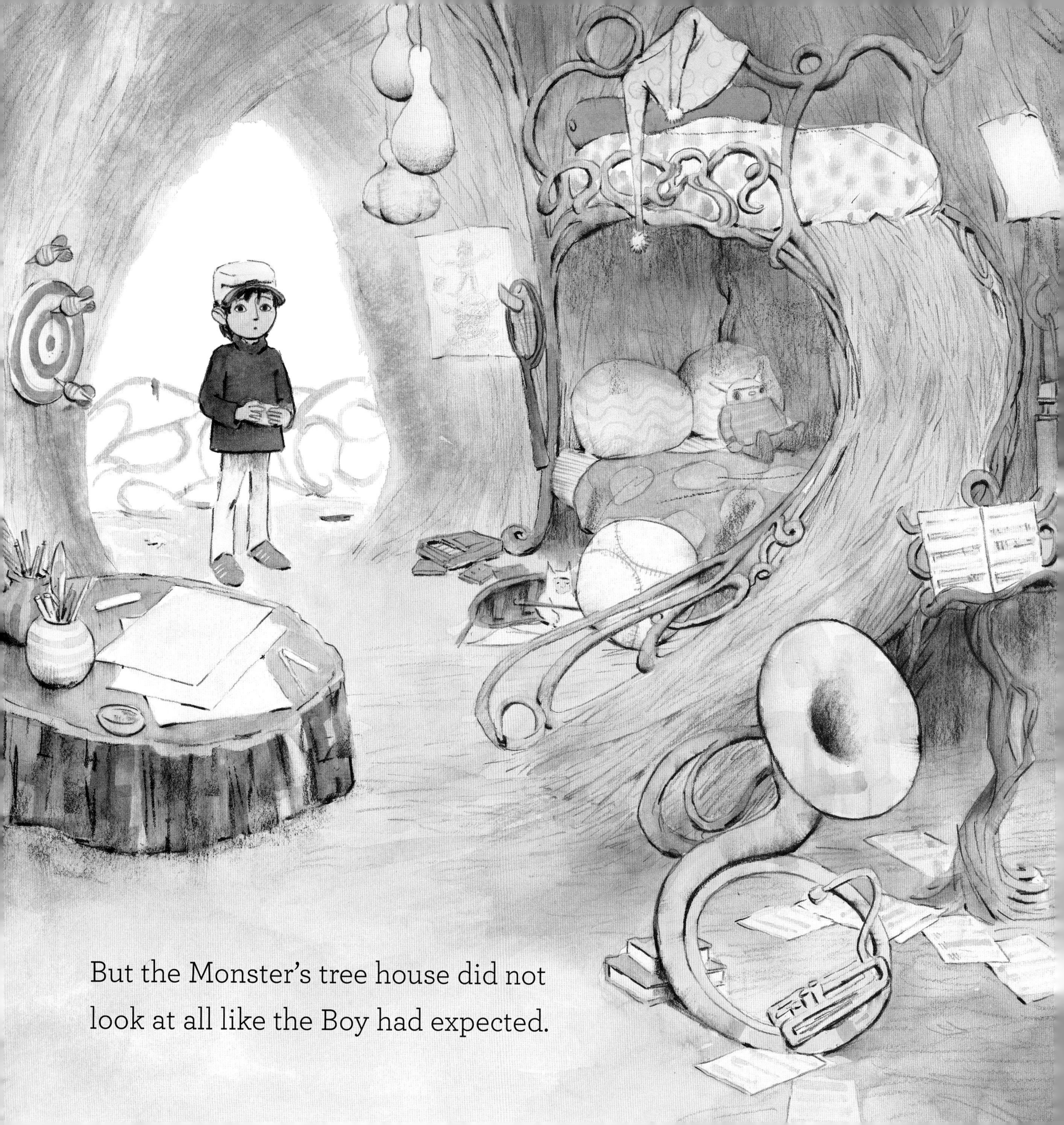

But the Monster's tree house did not look at all like the Boy had expected.

Hmm . . . Putting up the rope together *had* been fun.

And the Monster seemed to like music. Really, *really* like it.

And the Boy *did* start the water balloon fight, after all.

Actually, that had been pretty fun too.

Things looked different from over here.

The Boy read the note he had written, and put it back in his pocket.

He climbed down the tree,

and followed the trail of broken rope.
Maybe, he thought, he could re-tie it.

When he stood up, there was the Monster.
For a moment, it felt strange. But then,

said the Boy.